Forty Favorite Songs
for High Voice

JOHANNES BRAHMS

Edited and with an Introduction by
James Huneker

DOVER PUBLICATIONS, INC.
Mineola, New York

Bibliographical Note

This Dover edition, first published in 2004, is an unabridged republication of
Forty Songs by Johannes Brahms from the series *The Musicians Library,* original-
ly published by Oliver Ditson Company, 1903.

International Standard Book Number: 0-486-43577-6

Manufactured in the United States of America
Dover Publications, Inc., 31 East 2nd Street, Mineola, N.Y. 11501

CONTENTS

JOHANNES BRAHMS

THE composer Johannes Brahms was born at Hamburg, May 7, 1833. He died at Vienna, April 3, 1897. And as Louis Ehlert wrote: "It is characteristic of his nature that he was born in a Northern seaport and his father a contrabassist. Sea air and basses, these are the ground elements of his music. Nowhere is there to be found a Southern luxuriance, amid which golden fruits smile upon every bough, nor the superabundance that spreads its fragrant breath over hill and dale. Nor may there be met that enervating self-absorption, renunciation of effort or Southern brooding submission to fate. . . . Brahms neither dazzles nor does he conquer by assault. Slowly but surely he wins all those hearts that demand from art not only excitement but also that it be filled with sacred fire and endowed with the lovely proportions of the beautiful."

We shall see presently that if Brahms is often austere and self-contained in his instrumental music, he is the reverse in his songs. It was a primal error in criticism to range Brahms among the classicists. He is a romantic by nature; even his formal edifices, built as they are on Bach and Beethoven, depart widely from traditional outlines. A Brahms symphony is no more like a Schumann than a Beethoven symphony; it stands alone in its severe magnificence of mass and color. Ehlert wittily remarks: "We receive the impression that he feels with his head and thinks with his heart."

If the life of Chopin resolved itself into one overshadowing romance, if Tchaïkovsky's career was an enigma to his friends, what may be said of the uneventful record of Brahms's long years of industry? Truly his days were spent in labor, in the unremitting toil Art demands from her votaries, and truly his works are the foundations of his fame. No man devoted himself so absolutely to his art. It was a consecration. Like Beethoven, Brahms was a bachelor. We catch no glimpses of love disappointments, no tragic partings, no profound griefs except one—the filial regrets over the loss of his mother which culminated in that true temple of manly restrained sorrow and hope, the *German Requiem*. His father was a double-bass player in the Hamburg City Theatre and gave the boy Johannes his first instruction. Later Marxsen took him in hand, drilling him soundly in theory and piano playing. At fourteen he made his first public appearance, playing his own variations on a folk-song. In 1853 he went on a professional tour with Remenyi. He was then twenty, but so accomplished a musician that he transposed at sight the piano part of Beethoven's *Kreutzer Sonata* from A to B flat, the piano being a semitone below pitch.

His piano performances are said to have been brilliant and solid, and not without charm. He wrote for the instrument like a master. We may easily credit the astounding stories told of his memory displayed in the Bach and Beethoven scores. In 1853 Brahms met Joseph Joachim, the Hungarian violin virtuoso, and a lifelong friendship began. Joachim gave the youthful genius, whose powerful head and mobile mask predestined for him a great future, a letter to Robert Schumann. At Düsseldorf that same year he played to Schumann his Opus 1, the C major piano sonata which so impressed the elder composer that he wrote the historic criticism *New Paths*, and in a day Brahms became famous. No adulation, public or critical, could disturb the rhythms of the man's ambitions. He had determined to be Beethoven's successor in the domain of the symphony, and to that goal he marched without haste, without rest. He became conductor of Prince of Lippe-Detmold's orchestra. From 1858 to 1862 he remained in

Hamburg sedulously studying, and then went to Vienna, where he conducted the *Singakademie* until 1864. During the following five years Brahms lived in Hamburg, Zurich and Baden-Baden, making concert tours with Julius Stockhausen, the *Lieder* singer. He returned to Vienna in 1869, where, until 1874, he directed the orchestral concerts of the " Gesellschaft der Musikfreunde." Again he left Vienna, residing near Heidelberg. In 1878 he made Vienna his permanent home, not leaving it except on concert tours or for occasional trips to Italy.

Brahms won wealth, honors and content. His life was a simple one; its emotional experiences may be guessed in his music. His was not the impassioned, dramatic temperament of a Richard Wagner, against whom he was unfortunately pitted by such critical admirers as Eduard Hanslick. Homely in his tastes, hating notoriety, he led the existence of a prosperous *bourgeois*. He had a few intimate friends, and heartily disliked being "lionized." This trait possibly led him to decline the honor of a degree from Cambridge University in 1877. Rather unsocial and timid, he could come out of his shell and be caustically witty when he so desired. He usually spent his summers at Ischl, where he enjoyed chamber-music in his house. The record given us by his contemporaries proves Johannes Brahms to have been a great and a warm-hearted man.

II

It is not rashly premature to assign a place among the immortals to Brahms. Coming after the last of the belated romanticists, untouched by the fever of the theatre, a realist with imagination, both a classicist and a romanticist, he led music back into its proper channels by showing that a phenomenal sense of form and a mastery of polyphony, second only to Bach, are not incompatible with the faculty of uttering old things in a new way. Brahms is not a reactionary any more than is Richard Wagner. Neither of these men found what he looked for in modern music, so one harked back to Gluck and the Greeks, the other to Bach and Beethoven. Consider the massiveness of Brahms's tonal architecture; consider those structures erected after years of toil; regard the man's enormous fertility of ideas and his enormous patience in developing them; consider the ease with which he moves, shackled by the most difficult forms—not assumed for the mere sake of the difficulty, but because it was the only form in which he could successfully express himself; consider his leavening genius, his active geniality—a geniality that militates against pedantry, scholastic dryness and the arithmetic music of the *Kapellmeister*; consider also the powerful brain of this composer, and then realize that all great works of art are the arduous victories of great minds over great imaginations. Brahms ever consciously schooled his imagination.

He was his own severest critic. He worked slowly, he produced slowly, and, born contemplative rather than dramatic, he incurred the reproach of being phlegmatic, Teutonic, heavy and thick. There is enough sediment in his collected works to give the color of truth to this allegation; but from the richness and cloudiness of the ferment is drawn off the finest wine; and how fine, how incomparably stimulating, is a draught of this wine after the thin, acid, frothing and bubbling stuff concocted at every season's musical vintage! Brahms is a living reproach to the haste of a superficial generation. Whatever he wrought, he wrought in bronze and for time and not for the hour. He restored to music its formal beauty; he is the greatest symphonist in the constructive sense since Beethoven. He did not fill the symphony with as romantic a content as Schumann, but he never defaced or distorted its flowing contours. Above all, his themes are symphonic. Not a colorist like Berlioz or Liszt, he is one of the greatest masters of pure orchestral line that ever lived. He is accused of not scoring happily. The accusation is not untrue. Brahms does not display the same gracious sense of voicing the needs and capabilities of the orchestral army as Berlioz, Dvořák and Richard Strauss. His instrumentation is often drab and opaque; but his nobility of utterance, his remarkable eloquence and ingenuity in treatment, allied with the feeling for the appropriate hue, render one forgetful that he was not a painter of tones. He was first the thinker, and wrote as if to him the garb were naught, the pure form, all.

Brahms is the first composer since Beethoven to sound the note of the sublime in his orchestra. He has been called austere for this. He compassed sublimity at times; and to this is allied a rather forbidding quality, a want of commonplace sympathy, a lack of personal profile that made his music disliked by critic, amateur and professional. He never rendered any concession to popularity; indeed he often and perversely went out of his way to displease. The cheap, facile triumph he despised; he saw all Europe covered with second-rate men in music, and he noted that they pleased; their only excuse for living was to give cheap pleasure. This libertinism in art was abhorred by Brahms, for the naturally serious bent of his mind superinduced a species of puritanism. It is a sign of his great culture and flexible mental operations that he studied and admired Wagner.

When the printed list of Brahms's achievements in song, symphony and choral works of vast proportions is studied, amazement is evoked at the fertility and versatility of the man. It is not alone that he wrote four symphonies of surpassing power, two piano concertos, a violin concerto, a double concerto for violin and violoncello, songs, piano pieces, great set compositions like the *Song of Destiny, Rinaldo* and the *German Requiem*, duos, trios, quartets, quintets, sextets, all manners of combinations for wood, wind, strings, voices; it is really the sum total of high excellence, the stern unyielding adherence to ideals sometimes almost frostily inhuman, in a word, the logical, consistent and philosophical trend of the man's mind that forces homage. For half a century he pursued the beautiful in its most elusive and difficult form; pursued it when the fashions of the hour, day and year mocked at such undeviating devotion, when form was called old-fashioned, sobriety voted dull, and footlight passion had invaded music's realm and menaced it in its very stronghold—the symphony.

In a complete life of Johannes Brahms this trait of fidelity, this marvellous spiritual obstinacy, should be lovingly set forth. Because Brahms refused to challenge current tendencies in art and literature, it was believed that he held himself aloof from humanity, was a Brahmin of art, not a bard chanting its full-blooded wants and woes with full throat. Nothing could be wider of the mark. His music throbs with humanity, with its richest blood. He is the greatest contrapuntist after Bach, the greatest architectonist after Beethoven; yet in his songs he is nearly as naïve, as manly, as tender as Robert Burns. His topmost peaks are tremendously remote and glitter and gleam in a rarefied atmosphere; yet how intimate, how full of charm, of graciousness, are his lyrics!

Brahms's workmanship is well-nigh impeccable, his technical mastery of material as great as Beethoven's and only outstripped by Bach's. His contribution to the technics of rhythm is rich, and he has literally popularized the harmonic cross-relations, rediscovered the arpeggio and elevated it from the lowly position of an accompanying figure to an integer of the melodic phrase. He rescued the chord of the sixth from its Bellini and Verdi servitude, as did Wagner the essential turn. The sharp transitions in modulation, the sharpening of minor chords and sixths, the playing of common time against triple and the use of tonalities and rhythms vague, indeterminate and almost misleading are all truly Brahmsian, and enhance the structural values and beauty of his music. He is a wonderful variationist and has the gift of catching and imprisoning moods we call spiritual. Sobriety, earnestness, an intensity that is like the blow of a steam-hammer and a rich informing fantasy are his, a virile spirit and, as Ehlert says, his "art undoubtedly rests upon the golden background of Bach's purity and concentration."

III

Brahms wrote two hundred songs less four for solo voice and set the various verse of fifty-nine poets. He was not always careful in his selection of this verse, though his taste in matters literary seems to have been superior to Tchaïkovsky's. He did not display the same predilection for Heine as Schumann and Robert Franz, possibly because these two composers had chosen the best work of that poet. Impersonal as is Brahms in absolute music, he is sometimes given to the dolefully sentimental in his poetry. At times he is positively expansive in the real tearful Teutonic style. He loves the open air, the clouds, the grass, the lilacs. He is moved by a violet, and is youthfully fervid when under the balcony of his lyric lady-love twanging a guitar. The scholastic pessimism that intrudes occasionally in his instrumental music is often interrupted in his songs by bursts of humor, jesting, student gaiety. He is genuinely tender in *My Queen* and overflowing with emotion in the *Love Song* (*Minnelied*, Op. 71, No. 5). *In Summer Fields* (*Feldeinsamkeit*, Op. 86, No. 2) the atmosphere is wonderfully enticing. It is a glorious song. There is sly humor in the *Disappointed Serenader* (*Vergebliches Ständchen*, Op. 84, No. 4) and exquisite emotion in *A Thought like Music* (*Wie Melodien*, Op. 105, No. 1). In his very first songs Brahms made a standard that he has seldom surpassed. *Faithful Love* (*Liebestreu*, Op. 3, No. 1) is a song of noble ideas, nobly expressed. It has the familiar sombre key-color which we recognize later in *Love is for ever* (*Von ewiger Liebe*, Op. 43, No 1) and *Treachery* (*Verrath*, Op. 105, No. 5).

What songs are there in the wonderful song literature of Germany more fragrant with sweetness and unfeigned emotion than *That Night in May* (*Die Mainacht*, Op. 43, No. 2), *To the Nightingale* (*An die Nachtigall*, Op. 46, No. 4), or the *Cradle Song* (*Wiegenlied*, Op. 49, No. 4)? Brahms was peculiarly happy in his delineation of the naïve moods hidden in the native folk-songs. While he never quite reached the adorable simplicity of *Haidenröslein*, his *Little Sandman* (*Sandmännchen*) and other songs of this character are a close second to Schubert. He is also the interpreter of souls discouraged, of the aspirations of those whom sorrow has crushed.

His treatment of the voice is unaffected, though he often buries the vocal part in his piano symphony—to use an old-fashioned term. The web and woof of piano and song are here inextricably woven. Neither Schumann nor Franz has spun the pattern so closely; and yet the vocal quality is never lost, one is never too conscious of the piano accompaniment. Brahms writes flexibly for the voice and seems to divine the hidden meanings of the poet. He employs as it suits him the thorough composed and conventional song forms. Indeed he uses the old-fashioned repetition verse with tantalizing frequency. But he often develops harmonic surprises, as in the case of *My Queen* and *Faithful Love*. The entrance of the major mode in the latter song is like a triumphant flash of sunrise.

The present selection is a just representation of the Brahms song literature. Some of these numbers are difficult; none, not even those of simple structure, are easy; all make exacting demands upon the singer's intelligence, musicianship and emotional powers; and all contain beautiful music. Critical authorities may differ about the permanent qualities of Johannes Brahms's symphonic music, but there is little dispute over his right to rank with Schubert, Schumann and Franz as a great master of lyric art.

There are biographical sketches of Brahms by Reimann and Deiters; but the one by Louis Ehlert, in the volume entitled *From the Tone World*, is the most readable. *Recollections of Brahms* by Dietrich and Widmann has the personal element; and J. A. Fuller-Maitland in *Masters of German Music*, and W. H. Hadow's *Studies in Modern Music* [*Second Series*] will furnish the student with valuable material and critical commentary.

James Huneker

INDEX

Forty Favorite Songs

for High Voice

1

To the Children of Robert and Clara Schumann

THE LITTLE SANDMAN
(SANDMÄNNCHEN)

(Published in 1858)

(Original Key)

Author unknown

JOHANNES BRAHMS
Volks-Kinderlieder Nº 4

Andante

SINGSTIMME

1. Die Blü - me - lein sie schla - fen schon längst im Mon - den -
2. Vö - ge - lein sie san - gen so süss im Son - nen -
3. männ - chen kommt ge - schli - chen und guckt durch's Fen - ster
4. männ - chen aus dem Zim - mer es schläft mein Herz - chen

VOICE

1. The flow'r - ets all sleep sound - ly Be - neath the moon's bright
2. birds that sang so sweet - ly When noon day sun rose
3. see, the lit - tle sand - man At the win - dow shows his
4. ere the lit - tle sand - man Is man - y steps a -

PIANO

molto **p** *e dolce*

una corda

schein, sie ni - cken mit den Kö - pfen aus ih - ren Sten - ge - lein.
schein, sie sind zur Ruh ge - gan - gen in ih - re Nest - chen klein.
lein, ob ir - gend noch ein Lieb - chen nicht mag zu Bet - te sein.
fein, es ist gar fest ver - schlos - sen schon sein Guck - äu - ge - lein.

ray; They nod their heads to - geth - er And dream the night a - way.
high, With - in their nests are sleep - ing; Now night is draw - ing nigh.
head, And looks for all good chil - dren, Who ought to be in bed.
way, Thy pret - ty eyes, my dar - ling, Close fast un - til next day.

REFRAIN(*

Es rüt-telt sich der Blü-then-baum, er säu-selt wie im
Das Heim-chen in dem Aeh-ren-grund, es thut al-lein sich
Und wo er nur ein Kind-chen fand, streut er ihm in die Au-gen
Es leuch-tet Mor-gen mir Will-komm das Aeu-ge-lein so

The bud-ding trees wave to and fro, and mur-mur soft and
The crick-et as it moves a-long A-lone gives forth its
And, as each wea-ry pet he spies, Throws sand in-to its
But they shall ope at morn-ing's light And greet the sun-shine

Traum.
kund.
Sand.
fromm.

Schla - fe, schla - fe, schlaf' du mein Kin-de - lein!

low.
song.
eyes.
bright.

Sleep on! sleep on, sleep on, my lit-tle one!

lein!

2. Die
3. Sand-
4. Sand-

one!

2. The
3. Now-
4. And

To Bettina von Arnim

FAITHFUL LOVE
(LIEBESTREU)

(Published in 1854)

(Original Key)

ROBERT REINICK
Translated by Arthur Westbrook

JOHANNES BRAHMS, Op.3, Nº 1

Molto lento Very slowly *(Sehr langsam)*

VOICE

PIANO

"Drown thy   sor - row, thy sor -   row and
„O ver - senk', o ver-senk' dein___

grief,   my___ child,   In   the   sea,   man-ya   fath - om
Leid,   mein___ Kind,   in   die   See,   in   die   tie - fe

dreamily
pp (träumerisch)

down!"   Though   stones   will   sink   to   the
See."   Ein   Stein   wohl   bleibt   auf   des

word, my child: To the winds with it a -
nur ein Wort, in den Wind da - mit hin -

way!" Oh, Moth - er, tho' tem - pests can
aus." O Mut - ter, und split - tert der

shat - ter the rocks, Yet my troth will en - dure for
Fels auch im Wind, mei - ne Treu - e, die hält ihn

8

To Albert Dietrich

TRUE LOVE
(TREUE LIEBE)

(Published in 1854)

(Original Key)

FERRAND
Translated by Arthur Westbrook

JOHANNES BRAHMS, Op. 7, Nº 1

The wa - ters now spar - kle and
Die Was - ser um - spiel - ten ihr

flash at her feet; They whis - per re - un - ion a -
schmei - chelnd den Fuss, wie Träu - me von se - li - gen

round her. There calls to the maid - en a
Stun - - den; es zog sie zur Tie - fe mit

voice _____ from the deep: _____
stil - - ler Ge - walt; _____

12

To Albert Dietrich

THE HUNTSMAN
(PAROLE)

(Published in 1854)

(Original Key)

JOSEPH von EICHENDORFF (1788–1857)
Translated by Arthur Westbrook

JOHANNES BRAHMS, Op. 7, N⁰ 2

PIANO

1 She stood at her cham - ber
(2) in the mer - ry
1 Sie stand wohl am Fen - ster
(2) als der Früh - ling ge -

win - dow, And sad - ly braid - ed her hair. The
spring - time, When blos - soms were driv - en like snow, She
bo - gen und flocht sich trau - rig das Haar, der
kom - men, die Welt war von Blü - then ver - schneit, da

Hunts - man he was her lov - er; The
felt new hope___ re - turn - ing, And
Jä - ger war fort___ ge - zo - gen, der
hat sie ein Herz sich ge - nom - men, und

Hunts - man he was not there.___
in - to the green-wood did go.___
Jä - ger ihr Lieb - ster war.___
ging in die grü - ne Haid'.___

2 But
2 Und

3 She
3 Sie

14

To *Albert Dietrich*

MY MOTHER LOVES ME NOT
(DIE TRAUERNDE)

(Published in 1854)

(Original Key)

VOLKSLIED
(Swabian Folksong)
Translated by E. D'Esterre-Keeling

JOHANNES BRAHMS, Op.7, N° 5

1 My moth-er loves me not, An' no sweet-heart ha' I got;
2 Look! how the oth-ers dance, I nev-er get a chance.

1 Mei Mue-ter mag mi net; und kei Schatz han i net,
2 Ge-stern isch Kirch-weih g'wä, mi hot mer g'wis net g'seh,

Eh, why do I not die? What use am I?
Ev'n if I would dance now, I don't know how.
3 Let the three ro-ses blow

ei, wa-rum sterb i net, was thu i do?
denn mir isch's gar so weh, i tanz ja net.
3 Lasst die drei Ro-se stehn,

That by yon cross do grow: Knew ye, per-chance, the maid Who there is laid?
die an dem Kreu-zle blühn: hent ihr das Mäd-le kennt, die drun-ter liegt?

A MAIDEN ROSE AT EARLY DAWN
(VOM VERWUNDETEN KNABEN)

(Published in 1861)

(Original Key)

GERMAN FOLKSONG
Translated by Frederic Field Bullard

JOHANNES BRAHMS, Op. 14, Nº 2

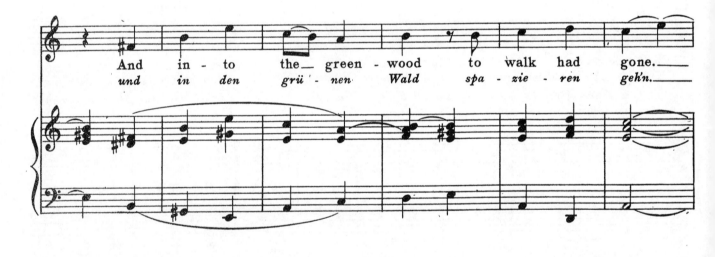

thee? / Till all the wa- ters reach the
geh'n? / Bis al - le Was - ser zu - sam - men

sea?_____ / To meet the wa - ters
geh'n?_____ / Ja, al - le Was - ser

nev - er wend, / And so my mourn-ing
geh'n nicht zu - sam'n, / so wird mein Trau - ern

dim.

can nev - er end._____
kein En - de han._____

TO AN AEOLIAN HARP
(AN EINE AEOLSHARFE)

(Published in 1862)

(Original Key)

EDUARD MÖRIKE (1804–1875)
Translated by Francis Hueffer and Arthur Westbrook

JOHANNES BRAHMS, Op. 19, Nº 5

26

sighed for. And, lo! a full-blown
Re - gung, *und hier,* *die vol - le*

rose - bush, soft - ly sha - ken, Has at my
Ro - se *streut* *ge - schüt - telt* *all' ih - re*

feet___ scat-ter'd all___ its pet - als!
Blät - ter vor mei - ne Fü - sse!

MY QUEEN
(WIE BIST DU MEINE KÖNIGIN)

(Composed in 1864)

(Original Key)

G. F. DAUMER (1800–1875)
Translated by Arthur Westbrook

JOHANNES BRAHMS, Op. 32, Nº 9
(1833–1897)

Ah, sweet my love, my gra-cious queen! As now, I've e'er thy sub-ject been.__ Dost thou but smile, then all a-round sweet Spring is smil-ing.

Wie bist du mei - ne Kö - ni - gin, durch sanf - te Gü - te won - ne voll:__ Du läch - le nur, Lenz - düf - te weh'n durch mein Ge - mü - the

queen, thou my queen.
voll, won - ne - voll.

Tho' I might roam in des-erts drear, All would be changed shoulds't thou ap-
Durch to - dte Wü - sten wan-dle hin, und grü - ne Schat - ten brei - ten

pear, Fra-grance and sweet re-fresh-ing shade Thou___ bring'st me
sich, ob fürch-ter - li - che Schwü-le dort ohn'___ En - de

ev - er, Thou my queen, thou my
brü - te, won - ne voll, won - ne -

To Julius Stockhausen

SLUMBER - SONG
(RUHE, SÜSSLIEBCHEN)

from the Magelone Cyclus

(Published in 1868)

(*Original Key*)

JOHANN LUDWIG TIECK (1778–1853)
Translated by John S. Dwight

JOHANNES BRAHMS, Op 33, № 9

Rest thee, my sweet, in the shad - ow Of the green - ly glim - mer - ing
Ru - he, Süss - lieb - chen, im Schat - ten der grü - nen, däm - mern - den

grove;—
Nacht;—

Soft sigh - eth the grass on the
es säu - selt das Gras auf den

mead - ow; Thou'rt fanned and art cooled in the shad - ow,
Mat - ten, es fä - chelt und kühlt dich der Schat - ten,

And watched by faith - ful love.
und treu - e Lie - be wacht.

Sleep,__ then, sleep on, 'Neath the
Schla - fe, schlaf' ein, lei - ser

whis - p'ring pine. Ev - er I'll be thine,
rauscht der Hain. E - wig bin ich dein,

poco cresc.

dim.

Ev - er, ev - er I'll _____ be
e - wig, e - wig bin _____ ich

thine.
dein.

p dolce

dim.

Hush ye! in - vis - i - ble cho - -
Schweigt, ihr ver - steck - ten Ge - sän - -

p dolce

rus! Dis - turb not her dain - ty re - pose! The
ge, und stört nicht die sü - sse - ste Ruh! Es

Whis - per low,_____ thou stream,_____ thou
rau - sche nur,_____ du stil - ler, du

purl - ing_____ stream! Charmed by
stil - ler_____ Bach. Schö - ne

some en - chant - ing vis - ion,
Lie - bes - phän - ta - sie - en

Full of all de - lights E - ly - sian,
spre - chen in den Me - lo - die - en,

Keep hum - ming to lull thee a -
und *sum* - *men* *zum Schlum* - *mer* *dich*

sleep, hum - ming to lull thee, to lull
ein, *sum* - *men zum Schlum - mer, zum Schlum* -

dim. *pp*

thee a - sleep.
mer dich ein.

p

dim. sempre e poco rit.

pp

LOVE IS FOR EVER
(VON EWIGER LIEBE)

(Published in 1868)

(Original Key, B)

JOS. WENTZIG
Translated by R.H.Benson, and Arthur Westbrook

JOHANNES BRAHMS, Op. 43, Nº 1

song of the lark; Yes, in the twi-light the home-steads are
nir - gend noch Rauch, ja, und die Ler - che sie schwei-get nun

dark.
auch.

p

Forth from the vil - lage the
Kommt aus dem Dor - fe der

lov - er is come, Guard-ing the maid-en and lead-ing her home;
Bur-sche her - aus, giebt das Ge - leit der Ge - lieb - ten nach Haus,

Choos-ing the path by the wil-lows a - part; Tell - ing her
führt sie an Wei - den-ge - bu-sche vor - bei, re - det so

42

Rather slowly *(Ziemlich langsam)*

And the maid - en an - swer - ed straight; "Our love shall
Spricht das Mäg-de-lein, Mäg - de - lein spricht: Un - se - re

pp dolce

nev - er be part - ed by fate: Strong____ tho' the steel and the
Lie - be, sie tren - net sich nicht! Fest____ ist der Stahl und das

un poco animato

un poco animato e

i - ron for aye,   Our   love is strong - er and sur - er than
Ei - sen gar sehr,   un - se - re Lie - be ist fe - ster noch

cresc.

mf

they.
mehr.

dim.

un poco rit.

I - ron and   steel can be sev - er'd in twain;   Our   love shall
Ei - sen und Stahl,___ man schmei - det sie um,   un - se - re

un poco animato

ev - er un - chan - ged re - main; I - ron and steel will not
Lie - be wer wan - delt sie um? Ei - sen und Stahl, sie

un poco animato e

p

al - way a - vail; Our love is plight - ed, our love is plight - ed and
kön - nen zer - gehn, un - se - re Lie - be, un - se - re Lie - be muss

cresc.

f

nev - ér, nev - er shall fail."
e - wig, e - - wig be - stehn!"

f

molto rit.

p

THAT NIGHT IN MAY
(DIE MAINACHT)

(Published in 1868)

(Original Key, E♭)

LUDWIG H.C.HÖLTY (1748–1776)
Translated by Frederic Field Bullard

JOHANNES BRAHMS, Op.43,№ 2

Sad - ly I wan - der from glade to glade.
wandl' ich trau - rig von Busch zu Busch.

Hid - ing there in the shade I hear the tur - tle-doves Soft - ly coo - ing of
Ü - ber - hül - let vom Laub gir - ret ein Tau - ben-paar sein Ent - zü - cken mir

love. Leav - ing them far be - hind,
vor; *a - ber ich wen - de mich,*

I press on to deep - er shad - - ows;
su - che dunk - le - re Schat - - ten,

And ___ I ___ weep for ut - ter ___ lone ___
und ___ die ___ ein - sa - me ___ Thrä ___

- li - ness.
- ne rinnt.

dim. rit.

When, O maid of my heart, Fair as the smil - ing morn
Wann, o lä - cheln - des Bild, wel - ches wie Mor - gen - roth

a tempo   *simile*

Thy love - ra - di - ant face When shall I look up - on?
durch die See - le mir strahlt, find' ich auf Er - den dich?

espressivo

See, the tears of my great lone - - - -
'nd die ein - sa - me Thrä - - - -

p cresc. legato

- - liness pour, burn - ing,
- ne bebt mir hei - sser,

mf

burn - - ing, my cheeks _____ a-
hei - - sser die Wang' _____ her-

p

long.
ab.

p   dim. rit.

TO THE NIGHTINGALE
(AN DIE NACHTIGALL)

(Published in 1868)

(Original Key)

H. von HÖLTY (1828-1887)
Translated by Frederic Field Bullard

JOHANNES BRAHMS, Op. 46, Nº 4

gale!
gall!

I hear the clear notes from thy sweet throat shak-en, And
Du tö - nest mir mit dei-ner sü - ssen Keh - le die

Love re - plies.
Lie - be wach;

Thy melt - ing meas-ures by-gone mem'ries waken
denn schon durch-bebt die Tie-fen mei-ner See-le

In won - drous wise,
dein schmel - zend Ach,

in
dein

won - - - drous wise.
schmel - - - zend Ach.

Then from my couch a - gain re - pose is ban - ished, And
Dann flieht der Schlaf von neu - em die - ses La - ger, ich

long I stare With tear - ful eye, from
star - re dann, mit nas - sem Blick und

which all hope has van - ished, To Heav -
tod - ten-bleich und ha - ger den Him -

- - en there. Go,
- - mel an. Fleuch,

THE WATCHFUL LOVER
(DER GANG ZUM LIEBCHEN)

(Published in 1868)

Bohemian Folksong.
Translated by Natalia Macfarren

(*Original Key, E minor*)

JOHANNES BRAHMS, Op. 48, Nº 1

Con grazia

VOICE

The moon in high heav-en the white clouds hath riv-en; I'll
Es glänzt der Mond nie-der, ich soll-te doch wie-der zu

PIANO

con Pedale

go to my dear one and stand at her door.
mei-nem Lieb-chen, wie mag es ihr geh'n?

animato

Sad vig-il she keep-eth, she sigh-eth and
Ach weh', sie ver-za-get und kla-get, und

animato

56

weep - eth, And thinks that in life she will ne'er see me more!
kla - get, dass sie ___ mich nim-mer im Le - ben wird seh'n!

Tempo I

The mo.on is near wa - ning; my
Es ging der Mond un - ter, ich

p

con Pedale

love is com - plain-ing; I'll has - ten and watch that no ri - val comes
eil - te doch mun-ter, und eil - te, dass kei - ner mein Lieb-chen ent -

nigh.
führt.

animato

animato

Ye doves I hear woo-ing, oh, cease from your coo-ing Un -
Ihr Täub - chen, o gir - ret, ihr Lüft - chen, o schwir-ret, dass

til to my dear one, my dear one I fly!
kei - ner mein Lieb-chen, mein Lieb - chen ent - führt!

TO A VIOLET
(AN EIN VEILCHEN)

(Published in 1868)

(Original Key)

H. von HÖLTY (1828-1887)
Translated by Arthur Westbrook

JOHANNES BRAHMS, Op. 49, Nº 2

Hide, O vio - let, with - in thine az - ure chal - ice— Hide these pale tears of sor -

Birg, o Veil - chen, in dei - nem blau - en Kel - che, birg die Thrä - nen der Weh -

row,
muth,

Till my
bis mein

true love finds thee here by the
Lieb - chen die - se Quel - le be -

brook!
sucht!

And if she,
Ent - pflückt sie

dolce

smil - ing,
lä - chelnd

bend to
dich dem

60

To B.F in Vienna

CRADLE SONG
(WIEGENLIED)

(Published in 1868)

(Original Key, Eb)

KARL SIMROCK (1802–1876)
Translated by Arthur Westbrook

JOHANNES BRAHMS, Op. 49, N° 4

Lul - la - by   and good night!   With__ ro - ses be - dight,__ Creep__ in - to thy__ bed,   There__ pil - low thy head.   If God will,   thou shalt

Gu - ten A - bend, gut' Nacht,   mit__ Ro - sen be - dacht,__ mit__ Näg - lein be - steckt   schlupf' un - ter die Deck: Mor - gen früh,   wenn Gott

blue eyes close tight;___ Bright an-gels are___ near, So___ sleep with - out
Eng' - lein be - wacht,___ die zei - gen im___ Traum dir___ Christ-kind - leins

fear. They will guard thee from harm With fair dream-land's sweet
Baum: Schlaf' nun se - lig und süss, schau' im Traum's Pa - ra

charm, They will guard thee from harm With fair dream-land's sweet charm.
dies, schlaf' nun se - lig und süss, schau' im Traum's Pa - ra - dies.

REMEMBRANCE
(ERINNERUNG)

(Published in 1874)

(Original Key)

MAX von SCHENKENDORF (1783–1817)
Translated by Frederic Field Bullard

JOHANNES BRAHMS, Op. 63, № 2

The fair - est maid be - neath the heav'n Once graced this
Ihr wun - der - schö - nen Au - gen - bli - cke, die Lieb - lich-

vale of pure de - light With her dear pres - ence and the
ste der gan - zen Welt hat euch mit ih - rem ew' - gen

fea - tures So bright and fair, so fair_____ and bright.
Glü - cke, mit ih - rem sü - ssen Licht_____ er - hellt.

68

spo - ken word! Your mag - ic charm can ne'er be
hauch - tes Wort, dein Zau - ber - bann wird nie ge -

bro - ken; Its sound and spell my soul_____ have stirred._____
bro -chen, du klingst und wir - kest fort_____ und fort._____

Tempo I

The fair - est maid be - neath the
Ihr wun - der - schö - nen Au - gen -

f

rit. e dim.

p legato

heav'n __ Once loved thee, vale of pure de - light. I gaze on
bli - cke, ihr lacht und lockt in ew - gem Reiz. Ich schau - e

thee with ten - der long -ing For her most pre - cious in __
sehn - suchts - voll zu - rü - cke voll Schmerz und Lust und Lie -

__ my sight.
- bes - geiz.

MY HEART IS IN BLOOM
(MEINE LIEBE IST GRÜN)
(Published in 1874)

(Original Key)

FERD. SCHUMANN
Translated by Frederic Field Bullard

JOHANNES BRAHMS, Op. 63, No. 5

With animation *(Lebhaft)*

VOICE

PIANO

Oh, my heart _____ is in bloom _____
Mei - ne Lie - - be ist grün _____

like the li - lac tree, And my
wie der Flie - der - busch, *und mein*

Love like a sun - beam _____ glow - eth, my
Lieb ist schön wie die Son - ne, *mein*

blow - - eth.
Won - - ne. string.

And my soul _____ has the wings _____
Mei - ne See - - le hat Schwin - -

joy of his per- fumed__ bow - ers, For
lie - bes - trun - ke - ne Lie - der, *viel*

joy of his per- fumed bow - -
lie - bes - trun - ke - ne Lie - -

ers.
der.

poco ten.

Ped.

OH, THAT I MIGHT RETRACE THE WAY
(O WÜSST' ICH DOCH DEN WEG ZURÜCK)

(Published in 1874)

KLAUS GROTH (1819–1899) (Original Key) JOHANNES BRAHMS, Op. 63, Nº 8

Rather slowly (*Etwas langsam*)

Oh, that I might re-trace the way, The
O wüsst' ich doch den Weg zu-rück, den

hap-py way to child-hood's land! A-far from home why
lie-ben Weg zum Kin-der-land! O wa-rum sucht' ich

did I stray, And leave my moth-er's hand, my moth-er's
nach dem Glück und liess der Mut-ter Hand, der Mut-ter

SONG OF THE SKYLARK

(LERCHENGESANG)

(Published in 1877)

(Original Key)

KARL CANDIDUS
Translated by Natalia Macfarren

JOHANNES BRAHMS, Op.70, Nº 2

LOVE SONG
(MINNELIED)

(Composed in 1877)

(Original Key)

H. HÖLTY (1828–1887)
Translated by Arthur Westbrook

JOHANNES BRAHMS, Op.71, Nº 5
(1833–1897)

With much tenderness but not too slowly
(Sehr innig doch nicht zu langsam)

Sweet-er
Hol - der

sounds the song of birds. When she roams the mead—ows, When she comes with step so
klingt der Vo - gel - sang, wenn die En - gel - rei - ne, die mein Jüng - lings herz be-

light, 'Mid—— the wood-land shad-ows.
zwang, wan - delt durch die Hai - ne.

me o'er-shad - ed.
schön und hei - ter.

Dear - est sov - 'reign of my
Trau - te, min - nig - li - che

heart, Leave, oh! leave me nev - er, Bloom sweet blos - soms of thy
Frau, wol - lest nim - mer flie - hen, dass mein Herz, gleich die - ser

love, In ___ my soul for ev - er, In my soul ___ for ev -
Au', mög' ___ in Won - ne ___ blü - hen, mög' in Won - ne blü - -

er.
hen.

THE QUIET WOOD
(O KÜHLER WALD)

(Published in 1877)

(Original Key, A♭)

CL. BRENTANO (1778-1842)
Translated by Frederic Field Bullard

JOHANNES BRAHMS, Op. 72, N? 3

Where shall I find the quiet wood In which my loved one strays? The echo soft where shall I seek, That knows and loves, The

O küh - ler Wald, wo rau - schest du, in dem mein Lieb - chen geht? O Wie - der - hall, wo lau - schest du, der gern mein Lied,

LAMENT
(VERZAGEN)

(Published in 1877)

(Original Key)

KARL LEMCKE
Translated by Frederic Field Bullard

JOHANNES BRAHMS, Op.72, Nº 4

breast!
where!
zu.
weh'n.

3 **O** rest - less, throb - bing
3 Du un - ge - stü - mes

cresc.

R. H.

L. H.

heart,
Herz,

Be
sei

still_____ and_____
still_____ und_____

give _____ my _____ spir - - it _____
gieb _____ dich _____ doch _____ zur _____

rest,
Ruh',

And know the storm - clouds and
du sollst mit Win - den und

bil - lows as kin - dred.
Wo - gen dich trö - sten,

Why art _____ thou so
was wei - nest, so was

sore _____ dis - trest?
wei - nest _____ du?

Ah,
was

Why _____ so _____ sore _____ dis -
wei - - *nest,* _____ *wei* - - *nest* _____

trest? _____
du? _____

THE DISAPPOINTED SERENADER
(VERGEBLICHES STÄNDCHEN)

(Published in 1882)

(Original Key)

Lower Rhine Folksong
Translated by Frederic Field Bullard

JOHANNES BRAHMS, Op.84, № 4

If you came in to__ me I would rue the day, I would rue,
wärst du her - ein mit__ Fug, wär's mit mir vor - bei, wär's mit mir,

I would rue, I would rue__ the day!
wär's mit mir, wär's mit mir__ vor - bei!

poco f

(He) The__ night is so cold,__ so chill - y the
(Er) So__ kalt ist die Nacht,__ so ei - sig der

wind, so chill - y the wind,
Wind, so ei - sig der Wind,

p

My heart will freeze right soon, And all my love be— gone.
dass mir das Herz er - friert, mein' Lieb' er - lö - schen wird,

Cru - el maid, be kind, cru - el maid, cru - el maid,
öff - ne mir, mein Kind, öff - ne mir, öff - ne mir,

Faster
(lebhafter)

cru - el maid, be kind! (She) Now if thy
öff - ne mir— mein Kind! (Sie) *Lö - schet dein'*

Più animato

love's go - ing, then let it go,
Lieb', lass sie lö - schen nur,

yes,   then   let ___ it   go!   Pray,   let   it
lass   sie   lö - schen   nur,   *Lö - schet   sie*

p leggiero

go   for ___ aye,   And   here   no   long - er ___ stay,   Pleas-ant dreams, young
im - mer ___ zu,   geh' heim   zu   Bett,   zur ___ Ruh,   gu - te   Nacht,   mein

man;   So, good night,   go   to   bed,   pleas-ant dreams, young
Knab',   gu - te   Nacht,   gu - te   Nacht,   gu - te   Nacht, ___   mein

man!
Knab'!

f.

sf

IN LONELY WOOD
(IN WALDESEINSAMKEIT)

(Published in 1882)

(Original Key)

KARL LEMCKE
Translated by Arthur Westbrook

JOHANNES BRAHMS, Op. 85, Nº 6

I once in si-lent wood-lands re-
Ich sass zu dei-nen Fü-ssen in

clined at thy dear side,
Wal - des-ein-sam-keit;

While the hill-winds,
Win - des - ath - men,

sigh ing, swept through the branch-es wide.
Seh - - nen ging durch die Wip-fel breit.

Up-
In

IN SUMMER FIELDS
(FELDEINSAMKEIT)

(Published in 1882)

(Original Key, F)

HERMANN ALMERS
Translated by Paul England (Verse I)
and Frederic Field Bullard (Verse II)

JOHANNES BRAHMS, Op.86, No.2

pure and ra-diant vi- sions, Like pure and ra-diant
schö - ne stil - le Träu - me, wie schö - ne stil - le

vi - sions. I feel the while as tho' I long were
Träu - me; mir ist, als ob ich längst ge-stor-ben

dolce.

dead, And borne on wings a - loft to fields E - ly - sian, And
bin, und zie - he se - lig mit durch ew' - ge Räu - me, und

borne on wings a -loft to fields E - ly - sian.
zie - he se - lig mit durch ew' - ge Räu - me.

pp

ARISE, BELOVED VISION
(STEIG' AUF, GELIEBTER SCHATTEN)

(Published in 1884)

(Original Key)

FRIEDRICH HALM
Translated by Frederic Field Bullard

JOHANNES BRAHMS, Op. 94, № 2

in_____ Thy might!   Liv - ing Thou hadst all
Nä - he Macht!   *Du hast's ge- konnt im*

dolce

pow - er—   In death all pow'r's still Thine.   To
Le - ben,   *du kannst es auch im Tod.*   *Sich*

p

tri - umph o - ver suf - f'ring Was Thy com - mand di -
nicht dem Schmerz er - ge - ben, war im - mer dein Ge-

108

SAPPHIC ODE
(SAPPHISCHE ODE)
(Published in 1884)

HANS SCHMIDT
Translated by Arthur Westbrook

(Original Key, D)

JOHANNES BRAHMS, Op. 94, Nº 4

Rather slowly *(Ziemlich langsam)*

Ro - ses culled at night from the dark -'ning
Ro - sen brach ich Nachts mir am dunk - len

hedge — rows Sweet - er than by day all their fragrance were breath - ing,
Ha - ge; Sü - sser hauch - ten Duft sie, als je — am Ta - ge;

Tho' the lad - en branch - es were mov - ing a - bove me,
Doch ver - streu - ten reich die be - weg - ten Ae - ste

Show — ers be - dew — ing.
Thau, — der mich näss - te.

So thy kiss-es' fra-grance as naught has
Auch der Küs - se Duft mich wie nie be-

charmed me, Kiss-es caught by night from thy lips'___ red blos-som;
rück - te, Die ich Nachts von Strauch dei-ner Lip - pen pflück - te:

Tho' from eyes with deep___ e-mo - tion glow - ing.
Doch auch dir be - wegt im Ge - müth___ gleich je - nen,

Tears _____ were flow - ing.
Thau - - ten die Thrä - nen.

MY EVERY THOUGHT IS WITH THEE, LOVE
(BEI DIR SIND MEINE GEDANKEN)

(Published in 1884)

(Original Key)

FRIEDRICH HALM
Translated by Frederic Field Bullard

JOHANNES BRAHMS, Op. 95, No 2

114

MAIDEN'S SONG
(MÄDCHENLIED)

(Published in 1884)

(*Original Key*)

PAUL HEYSE (1830 -
(after the Italian)
Translated by Frederic Field Bullard

JOHANNES BRAHMS, Op.95, No 6

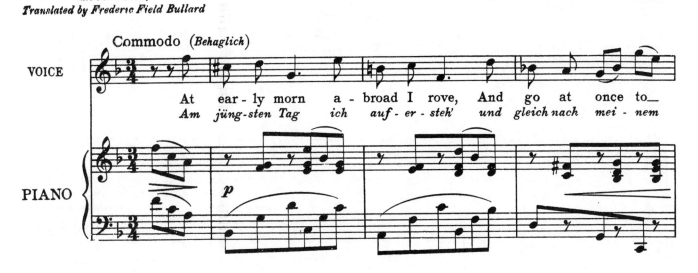

Commodo (*Behaglich*)

VOICE

PIANO

At ear-ly morn a-broad I rove, And go at once to
Am jüng-sten Tag ich auf-er-steh' und gleich nach mei-nem

seek my Love: And if my Love I do not meet,
Lieb-sten seh', und wenn ich ihn nicht fin-den kann,

poco rit.

I hie me back to slum-ber sweet, I hie me back to slum-ber
leg' wie-der mich zum Schla-fen dann, leg' wie-der mich zum Schla-fen

dim. *poco rit.*

116

sweet.
dann.

What grief is ours, what end-less pain, Till,
O Her - ze - leid, du E - wig-keit. Selb -

hand in hand, we meet a - gain!
an - der nur ist Se - lig-keit!

And, if my Love cast
Und kommt mein Lieb - ster

out__ should be, There'll be no Par - a - dise for__ me,__ there'll be no
nicht hin - ein, mag nicht im Pa - ra - die - se__ sein,__ mag nicht im

Par - a - dise__ for me!
Pa - ra - die - se sein.

OH, DEATH IS LIKE THE COOLING NIGHT
(DER TOD, DAS IST DIE KÜHLE NACHT)

(Composed in 1886)

(Original Key)

HEINRICH HEINE (1799-1856)
Translated by Frederic Field Bullard

JOHANNES BRAHMS, Op. 96, No 1

118

hear him, I hear him e'en while I
hör' es, ich hör' es so - gar im

dream, e'en while I dream.
Traum, so - gar im Traum.

più p

p

NIGHTINGALE
(NACHTIGALL)

(Published in 1886)

(*Original Key*)

C. REINHOLD
Translated by Frederic Field Bullard

JOHANNES BRAHMS, Op. 97, № 1

Nay, wee, wise song-ster, nay;___ What brings this
Nein, trau-ter Vo-gel, nein!___ was in mir

hap-py pain to-day Is not thy lay.___ It comes from
schafft so sü-sse Pein, das ist nicht dein,___ das ist von

ac - - cents deep and ring - ing, Which long were
an - - dern, him-mel - schö - nen, nun längst für

si - lent in my— sing - ing, And soft - ly now re -
mich ver - klun - ge - nen Tö - nen, in dei - nem Lied ein

ech - o in thy lay,
lei - ser Wie - der - hall,

re - ech - o in thy lay.
ein lei - ser Wie - der - hall!

A BIRD FLIES OVER THE RHINE
(AUF DEM SCHIFFE)

(Published in 1886)

(Original Key)

C. REINHOLD
Translated by Frederic Field Bullard

JOHANNES BRAHMS, Op. 97, No. 2

A lit - tle bird flies o - ver the
Ein Vö - ge - lein fliegt ü - ber den

Rhine   And   flut - ters   his   wings   in   the   glad   sun -
Rhein   und   wiegt___   die   Flü - gel   im   Son   nen -

shine;   Sees   vine -   clad
schein,   sieht   Re -   ben

hills   and   the   riv -   er   green,   In   gold -   en
hü - gel   und   grü -   ne   Fluth   in   gold'ner

sheen,___ in gold - en sheen.
Gluth,___ in gold' - ner Gluth.

How hap - py he, how hap - - py
Wie wohl das thut, wie wohl ___ das

he, ___ On high ___ up - lift - ed at
thut, ___ so hoch ___ er - ho - ben im

morn ___ to ___ be! ___
Mor - gen hauch!

COME SOON
(KOMM BALD)

(Published in 1886)

(Original Key)

KLAUS GROTH, (1819 – 1899)
Translated by Frederic Field Bullard

JOHANNES BRAHMS, Op. 97, Nº 5

DO YOU OFTEN CALL TO MIND?
(KOMMT DIR MANCHMAL IN DEN SINN?)

(From Gipsy Songs)

(Zigeunerlieder)

(Published in 1888)

(Original Key)

German text by HUGO CONRAT
from the Hungarian
Translated by Arthur Westbrook

JOHANNES BRAHMS, Op.103, № 7

Do you oft - en call to mind, my on - ly love,
Kommt dir manch-mal in den Sinn, mein sü - sses Lieb,

What you prom - ised once-the ho - ly
was du einst mit heil' - gem Ei - de

vows you made?
mir ge - lobt?

Do you oft - en
Kommt dir manch - mal

call to mind, my on - ly love,
in den Sinn, mein sü - sses Lieb,

What you prom - ised once— the ho - ly vows you made?
was du einst mit heil' - gem Ei - de mir ge - lobt?

Leave me not! For - sake me not!
Täusch' mich nicht, ver - lass mich nicht,

mp

You know not how dear-ly I love thee;
du weisst nicht wie lieb___ ich dich hab',

cresc.

Love me then, as I love you___ And the smile of
lieb' du mich___ wie ich dich,___ dann strömt Got - tes

God shall bless us two.
Huld auf dich her - ab!

dolce

A THOUGHT LIKE MUSIC
(WIE MELODIEN ZIEHT ES MIR)
(Composed in 1889)

(Original Key, A)

KLAUS GROTH (1819 -
Translated by Isabella G. Parker.

JOHANNES BRAHMS, Op.105, No.1
(1833-1897)

A thought, like mu - sic,___ hold - ing My
Wie Me - lo - di - en___ zieht es mir

heart in soft con - trol, Like flow'rs of spring un -
lei - se durch den Sinn, Wie Früh - lings - blu - men

fold - ing, It thrill - eth through my soul,
blüht es und schwebt wie Duft da - hin,

It thrill - eth through my soul.
und schwebt wie Duft da - hin.

But if a word be spo - ken, Its beau - ty to con -
Doch kommt das Wort und fasst es und führt es vor das

vey, The spell at once is bro - ken, 'Twill
Aug; Wie Ne - bel - grau er - blasst es und

van - ish quite a - way, 'Twill
schwin - det wie ein Hauch, und

van - ish quite a - way.
schwin - det wie ein Hauch.

In mel - o - dy___ deep___
Und den - noch ruht___ im

hid - den, A fra - grance lies con - ceal'd, That
Rei - me ver - bor - gen wohl ein Duft, Den

bring - eth tears un - bid - den; Un -
mild aus stil - lem Kei - me ein

dim.

LIGHTER FAR IS NOW MY SLUMBER
(IMMER LEISER WIRD MEIN SCHLUMMER)

(Published in 1889)

(*Original Key, C♯*)

HERMANN LINGG
Translated by Frederic Field Bullard

JOHANNES BRAHMS, Op.105, № 2

dreams thy voice a - gain Call - eth to me ten - der - ly;
Trau - me hör' ich dich ru - fen d'raus vor mei - ner Thür,

But the door is closed to thee:
Nie - mand wacht und öff - net dir,

Then I wake and weep for bit - ter pain, bit -
ich er - wach' und wei - ne bit - ter - lich, wei -

- ter, bit - ter pain.
- ne bit - ter - lich.

TREACHERY
(VERRATH)

(Published in 1889)

(Original Key, B minor)

KARL LEMCKE
Translated by Arthur Westbrook

JOHANNES BRAHMS, Op. 105, Nº 5

tor - rent swift was flow - ing, was flow - ing.
Giess - bach floss ge - schwin - de, ge - schwin - de.

The lin - dens near a cot - tage grew; I heard the door-hinge
Die Lin - de stand vor Lieb - chens Haus, die Thü - re hört ich

grat - ing. My false love let a stran - ger out, And
knar - ren. Mein Schatz liess sacht ein Manns - bild 'raus: Lass

As at the beginning
(Wie zu Anfang)

And
Und

when the rud - dy, glow-ing sun A - rose up - on the mor - - row,
als er-schien der lich - te Tag, was fand er auf der Hai - de?

A corpse 'mid tramp led blos-soms lay, To that false maid - en's
Ein Tod - ter in den Blu - men lag zu ei - ner Fal - schen

sor - - row, to her sor - - - row.
Lei - de, ja Lei - - de.

SERENADE
(STÄNDCHEN)

(Published in 1889)

(Original Key)

FRANZ KUGLER
Translated by Frederic Field Bullard

JOHANNES BRAHMS, Op.106, No.1

The moon hangs o - ver the hill - tops, And now is the time for love.____
*Der Mond steht ü - ber dem Ber - ge,' so recht für ver - lieb - te Leut;*____

A foun - tain plays in the gar - den. No
im Gar - ten rie - selt eie Brun - nen, sonst

crea - ture , there____ doth move:
Stil - le , weit____ und breit.

Till____ to the foot of the ter - race
Ne - ben der Mau - er ' im Schat - ten,
(pp)

Three stu - dents come in the
da steh'n____ der Stu-den - ten

shade, With man - do - lins and a zith - er, A -
drei, mit Flöt'____ und Geig'____ und Zi - ther, und

151

THE FROST WAS WHITE
(ES HING DER REIF)

(Published in 1889)

(Original Key)

KLAUS GROTH (1819-1899)
Translated by Frederic Field Bullard

JOHANNES BRAHMS, Op.106, № 3

MY SONGS
(MEINE LIEDER)

(Published in 1889)

(Original Key)

ADOLF FREY
Translated by Frederic Field Bullard

JOHANNES BRAHMS, Op. 106, N° 4

Spirited and soft *(Bewegt und leise)*

PIANO

p
dolce

When my heart in po - et -
Wenn mein Herz be - ginnt zu

mad - ness With a song would
klin - gen und den Tö - nen

tell its glad - ness,
lösst die Schwin - gen,

dolce

Dover Opera, Choral and Lieder Scores

Bach, Johann Sebastian, ELEVEN GREAT CANTATAS. Full vocal-instrumental score from Bach-Gesellschaft edition. *Christ lag in Todesbanden, Ich hatte viel Bekümmerniss, Jauchhzet Gott in allen Landen,* eight others. Study score. 350pp. 9 χ 12. 23268-9

Bach, Johann Sebastian, MASS IN B MINOR IN FULL SCORE. The crowning glory of Bach's lifework in the field of sacred music and a universal statement of Christian faith, reprinted from the authoritative Bach-Gesellschaft edition. Translation of texts. 320pp. 9 x 12. 25992-7

Bach, Johann Sebastian, SEVEN GREAT SACRED CANTATAS IN FULL SCORE. Seven favorite sacred cantatas. Printed from a clear, modern engraving and sturdily bound; new literal line-for-line translations. Reliable Bach-Gesellschaft edition. Complete German texts. 256pp. 9 x 12. 24950-6

Bach, Johann Sebastian, SIX GREAT SECULAR CANTATAS IN FULL SCORE. Bach's nearest approach to comic opera. *Hunting Cantata, Wedding Cantata, Aeolus Appeased, Phoebus and Pan, Coffee Cantata,* and *Peasant Cantata.* 286pp. 9 x 12. 23934-9

Beethoven, Ludwig van, FIDELIO IN FULL SCORE. Beethoven's only opera, complete in one affordable volume, including all spoken German dialogue. Republication of C. F. Peters, Leipzig edition. 272pp. 9 x 12. 24740-6

Beethoven, Ludwig van, SONGS FOR SOLO VOICE AND PIANO. 71 lieder, including "Adelaide," "Wonne der Wehmuth," "Die ehre Gottes aus der Natur," and famous cycle *An die ferne Geliebta.* Breitkopf & Härtel edition. 192pp. 9 x 12. 25125-X

Bizet, Georges, CARMEN IN FULL SCORE. Complete, authoritative score of perhaps the world's most popular opera, in the version most commonly performed today, with recitatives by Ernest Guiraud. 574pp. 9 x 12. 25820-3

Brahms, Johannes, COMPLETE SONGS FOR SOLO VOICE AND PIANO (two volumes). A total of 113 songs in complete score by greatest lieder writer since Schubert. Series I contains 15-song cycle *Die Schone Magelone;* Series II includes famous "Lullaby." Total of 448pp. 9⅜ x 12¼.
Series I: 23820-2
Series II: 23821-0

Brahms, Johannes, COMPLETE SONGS FOR SOLO VOICE AND PIANO: Series III. 64 songs, published from 1877 to 1886, include such favorites as "Geheimnis," "Alte Liebe," and "Vergebliches Standchen." 224pp. 9 x 12. 23822-9

Brahms, Johannes, COMPLETE SONGS FOR SOLO VOICE AND PIANO: Series IV. 120 songs that complete the Brahms song oeuvre, with sensitive arrangements of 91 folk and traditional songs. 240pp. 9 x 12. 23823-7

Brahms, Johannes, GERMAN REQUIEM IN FULL SCORE. Definitive Breitkopf & Härtel edition of Brahms's greatest vocal work, fully scored for solo voices, mixed chorus and orchestra. 208pp. 9⅜ x 12¼. 25486-0

Debussy, Claude, PELLÉAS ET MÉLISANDE IN FULL SCORE. Reprinted from the E. Fromont (1904) edition, this volume faithfully reproduces the full orchestral-vocal score of Debussy's sole and enduring opera masterpiece. 416pp. 9 x 12. (Available in U.S. only) 24825-9

Debussy, Claude, SONGS, 1880–1904. Rich selection of 36 songs set to texts by Verlaine, Baudelaire, Pierre Louÿs, Charles d'Orleans, others. 175pp. 9 x 12. 24131-9

Fauré, Gabriel, SIXTY SONGS. "Clair de lune," "Apres un reve," "Chanson du pecheur," "Automne," and other great songs set for medium voice. Reprinted from French editions. 288pp. 8⅜ x 11. (Not available in France or Germany) 26534-X

Gilbert, W. S. and Sullivan, Sir Arthur, THE AUTHENTIC GILBERT & SULLIVAN SONGBOOK, 92 songs, uncut, original keys, in piano renderings approved by Sullivan. 399pp. 9 x 12. 23482-7

Gilbert, W. S. and Sullivan, Sir Arthur, HMS PINAFORE IN FULL SCORE. New edition by Carl Simpson and Ephraim Hammett Jones. Some of Gilbert's most clever flashes of wit and a number of Sullivan's most charming melodies in a handsome, authoritative new edition based on original manuscripts and early sources. 256pp. 9 x 12. 42201-1

Gilbert, W. S. and Sullivan, Sir Arthur (Carl Simpson and Ephraim Hammett Jones, eds.), THE PIRATES OF PENZANCE IN FULL SCORE. New performing edition corrects numerous errors, offers performers the choice of two versions of the Act II finale, and gives the first accurate full score of the "Climbing over Rocky Mountain" section. 288pp. 9 x 12. 41891-X

Hale, Philip (ed.), FRENCH ART SONGS OF THE NINETEENTH CENTURY: 39 Works from Berlioz to Debussy. 39 songs from romantic period by 18 composers: Berlioz, Chausson, Debussy (six songs), Gounod, Massenet, Thomas, etc. French text, English singing translation for high voice. 182pp. 9 x 12. (Not available in France or Germany) 23680-3

Handel, George Frideric, GIULIO CESARE IN FULL SCORE. Great Baroque masterpiece reproduced directly from authoritative Deutsche Handelgesellschaft edition. Gorgeous melodies, inspired orchestration. Complete and unabridged. 160pp. 9⅜ x 12¼. 25056-3

Handel, George Frideric, MESSIAH IN FULL SCORE. An authoritative full-score edition of the oratorio that is the best-known, most-beloved, most-performed large-scale musical work in the English-speaking world. 240pp. 9 x 12. 26067-4

Lehar, Franz, THE MERRY WIDOW: Complete Score for Piano and Voice in English. Complete score for piano and voice, reprinted directly from the first English translation (1907) published by Chappell & Co., London. 224pp. 8⅜ x 11¼. (Available in U.S. only) 24514-4

Liszt, Franz, THIRTY SONGS. Selection of extremely worthwhile though not widely-known songs. Texts in French, German, and Italian, all with English translations. Piano, high voice. 144pp. 9 x 12. 23197-6

Monteverdi, Claudio, MADRIGALS: BOOK IV & V. 39 finest madrigals with new line-for-line literal English translations of the poems facing the Italian text. 256pp. 8⅛ x 11. (Available in U.S. only) 25102-0

Moussorgsky, Modest Petrovich, BORIS GODUNOV IN FULL SCORE (Rimsky-Korsakov Version). Russian operatic masterwork in most-recorded, most-performed version. Authoritative Moscow edition. 784pp. 8⅜ x 11¼. 25321-X

Mozart, Wolfgang Amadeus, THE ABDUCTION FROM THE SERAGLIO IN FULL SCORE. Mozart's early comic masterpiece, exactly reproduced from the authoritative Breitkopf & Härtel edition. 320pp. 9 x 12. 26004-6

Mozart, Wolfgang Amadeus, COSI FAN TUTTE IN FULL SCORE. Scholarly edition of one of Mozart's greatest operas. Da Ponte libretto. Commentary. Preface. Translated Front Matter. 448pp. 9⅜ x 12¼. (Available in U.S. only) 24528-4

Available from your music dealer or write for free Music Catalog to
Dover Publications, Inc., Dept. MUBI, 31 East 2nd Street, Mineola, NY 11501
Visit us online at www.doverpublications.com

Dover Opera, Choral and Lieder Scores

Mozart, Wolfgang Amadeus, DON GIOVANNI: COMPLETE ORCHESTRAL SCORE. Full score that contains everything from the original version, along with later arias, recitatives, and duets added to original score for Vienna performance. Peters edition. Study score. 468pp. 9⅜ x 12¼. (Available in U.S. only) 23026-0

Mozart, Wolfgang Amadeus, THE MAGIC FLUTE (DIE ZAUBERFLÖTE) IN FULL SCORE. Authoritative C. F. Peters edition of Mozart's brilliant last opera still widely popular. Includes all the spoken dialogue. 226pp. 9 x 12. 24783-X

Mozart, Wolfgang Amadeus, THE MARRIAGE OF FIGARO: COMPLETE SCORE. Finest comic opera ever written. Full score, beautifully engraved, includes passages often cut in other editions. Peters edition. Study score. 448pp. 9⅜ x 12¼. (Available in U.S. only) 23751-6

Mozart, Wolfgang Amadeus, REQUIEM IN FULL SCORE. Masterpiece of vocal composition, among the most recorded and performed works in the repertoire. Authoritative edition published by Breitkopf & Härtel, Wiesbaden. 203pp. 8⅜ x 11¼. 25311-2

Offenbach, Jacques, OFFENBACH'S SONGS FROM THE GREAT OPERETTAS. Piano, vocal (French text) for 38 most popular songs: *Orphée, Belle Hélène, Vie Parisienne, Duchesse de Gérolstein,* others. 21 illustrations. 195pp. 9 x 12. 23341-3

Puccini, Giacomo, LA BOHÈME IN FULL SCORE. Authoritative Italian edition of one of the world's most beloved operas. English translations of list of characters and instruments. 416pp. 8⅜ x 11¼. (Not available in United Kingdom, France, Germany or Italy) 25477-1

Rossini, Gioacchino, THE BARBER OF SEVILLE IN FULL SCORE. One of the greatest comic operas ever written, reproduced here directly from the authoritative score published by Ricordi. 464pp. 8⅜ x 11¼. 26019-4

Schubert, Franz, COMPLETE SONG CYCLES. Complete piano, vocal music of *Die Schöne Müllerin, Die Winterreise, Schwanengesang.* Also Drinker English singing translations. Breitkopf & Härtel edition. 217pp. 9⅜ x 12¼. 22649-2

Schubert, Franz, SCHUBERT'S SONGS TO TEXTS BY GOETHE. Only one-volume edition of Schubert's Goethe songs from authoritative Breitkopf & Härtel edition, plus all revised versions. New prose translation of poems. 84 songs. 256pp. 9⅜ x 12¼. 23752-4

Schubert, Franz, 59 FAVORITE SONGS. "Der Wanderer," "Ave Maria," "Hark, Hark, the Lark," and 56 other masterpieces of lieder reproduced from the Breitkopf & Härtel edition. 256pp. 9⅜ x 12¼. 24849-6

Schumann, Robert, SELECTED SONGS FOR SOLO VOICE AND PIANO. Over 100 of Schumann's greatest lieder, set to poems by Heine, Goethe, Byron, others. Breitkopf & Härtel edition. 248pp. 9⅜ x 12¼. 24202-1

Strauss, Richard, DER ROSENKAVALIER IN FULL SCORE. First inexpensive edition of great operatic masterpiece, reprinted complete and unabridged from rare, limited Fürstner edition (1910) approved by Strauss. 528pp. 9⅜ x 12¼. (Available in U.S. only) 25498-4

Strauss, Richard, DER ROSENKAVALIER: VOCAL SCORE. Inexpensive edition reprinted directly from original Fürstner (1911) edition of vocal score. Verbal text, vocal line and piano "reduction." 448pp. 8⅜ x 11¼. (Not available in Europe or the United Kingdom) 25501-8

Strauss, Richard, SALOME IN FULL SCORE. Atmospheric color predominates in composer's first great operatic success. Definitive Fürstner score, now extremely rare. 352pp. 9⅜ x 12¼. (Available in U.S. only) 24208-0

Verdi, Giuseppe, AÏDA IN FULL SCORE. Verdi's glorious, most popular opera, reprinted from an authoritative edition published by G. Ricordi, Milan. 448pp. 9 x 12. 26172-7

Verdi, Giuseppe, FALSTAFF. Verdi's last great work, his first and only comedy. Complete unabridged score from original Ricordi edition. 480pp. 8⅜ x 11¼. 24017-7

Verdi, Giuseppe, OTELLO IN FULL SCORE. The penultimate Verdi opera, his tragic masterpiece. Complete unabridged score from authoritative Ricordi edition, with Front Matter translated. 576pp. 8¼ x 11. 25040-7

Verdi, Giuseppe, REQUIEM IN FULL SCORE. Immensely popular with choral groups and music lovers. Republication of edition published by C. F. Peters, Leipzig. Study score. 204pp. 9⅜ x 12¼. (Available in U.S. only) 23682-X

Wagner, Richard, DAS RHEINGOLD IN FULL SCORE. Complete score, clearly reproduced from B. Schott's authoritative edition. New translation of German Front Matter. 328pp. 9 x 12. 24925-5

Wagner, Richard, DIE MEISTERSINGER VON NÜRNBERG. Landmark in history of opera, in complete vocal and orchestral score of one of the greatest comic operas. C. F. Peters edition, Leipzig. Study score. 823pp. 8⅛ x 11. 23276-X

Wagner, Richard, DIE WALKÜRE. Complete orchestral score of the most popular of the operas in the Ring Cycle. Reprint of the edition published in Leipzig by C. F. Peters, ca. 1910. Study score. 710pp. 8⅜ x 11¼. 23566-1

Wagner, Richard, THE FLYING DUTCHMAN IN FULL SCORE. Great early masterpiece reproduced directly from limited Weingartner edition (1896), incorporating Wagner's revisions. Text, stage directions in English, German, Italian. 432pp. 9⅜ x 12¼. 25629-4

Wagner, Richard, GÖTTERDÄMMERUNG. Full operatic score, first time available in U.S. Reprinted directly from rare 1877 first edition. 615pp. 9⅜ x 12¼. 24250-1

Wagner, Richard, LOHENGRIN IN FULL SCORE. Wagner's most accessible opera. Reproduced from first engraved edition (Breitkopf & Härtel, 1887). 295pp. 9⅜ x 12¼. 24335-4

Wagner, Richard, PARSIFAL IN FULL SCORE. Composer's deeply personal treatment of the legend of the Holy Grail, renowned for splendid music, glowing orchestration. C. F. Peters edition. 592pp. 8⅛ x 11. 25175-6

Wagner, Richard, SIEGFRIED IN FULL SCORE. *Siegfried,* third opera of Wagner's famous Ring Cycle, is reproduced from first edition (1876). 439pp. 9⅜ x 12¼. 24456-3

Wagner, Richard, TANNHAUSER IN FULL SCORE. Reproduces the original 1845 full orchestral and vocal score as slightly amended in 1847. Included is the ballet music for Act I written for the 1861 Paris production. 576pp. 8⅜ x 11¼. 24649-3

Wagner, Richard, TRISTAN UND ISOLDE. Full orchestral score with complete instrumentation. Study score. 655pp. 8⅛ x 11. 22915-7

von Weber, Carl Maria, DER FREISCHÜTZ. Full orchestral score to first Romantic opera, forerunner to Wagner and later developments. Still very popular. Study score, including full spoken text. 203pp. 9 x 12. 23449-5

Wolf, Hugo, THE COMPLETE MÖRIKE SONGS. Splendid settings to music of 53 German poems by Eduard Mörike, including "Der Tambour," "Elfenlied," and "Verborganheit." New prose translations. 208pp. 9⅜ x 12¼. 24380-X

Wolf, Hugo, SPANISH AND ITALIAN SONGBOOKS. Total of 90 songs by great 19th-century master of the genre. Reprint of authoritative C. F. Peters edition. New Translations of German texts. 256pp. 9⅜ x 12¼. 26156-5

*Available from your music dealer or write for **free** Music Catalog to*
Dover Publications, Inc., Dept. MUBI, 31 East 2nd Street, Mineola, NY 11501
*Visit us online at **www.doverpublications.com***